HOUSE PAINT & OTHER STORIES

Felstead and Waddell

House Paint and Other Stories
© Felstead and Waddell

All illustrations by Tony Felstead

Cover and book design by Charlie De Grussa

Proofread by Jo Alderson

Performance photographs by Natasha Bidgood

A CIP Catalogue for this book is available
from the British Library.

ISBN 9781907590313

First published in 2014 by Thinking Ink Limited,
Media House, Suite 32, Brighton, BN2 3HA

To our families, thank you

ONE HUNDRED WORDS OF FOREWORD FROM COLIN GRANT

I scratch my head at a Felstead and Waddell story. What is it, really? It seems to lie somewhere between haiku poetry and snapshot prose. Watching the peculiar stories dramatised by the pair on stage it's as if Vladimir and Estragon, fed up with waiting for Godot, had wandered into a cabaret. The illustrated Felstead and Waddell one hundred word stories conjure a wonderland that is wryly unsettling: a flat with one door is exited by the window; a cactus replaces its owner. What's the meaning of these enigmatic modern day fables? Anything? Nothing? Everything? I'm still trying to find out.

HOUSE PAINT

I love my house. I have lived in it for sixteen years. It is a big house and it has lots of rooms. I have painted them all white. Sometimes, things go wrong in my house and things get broken. When this happens I go to the nearest DIY shop and I buy some white paint. Then I take my white paint home and I paint over the thing that is broken. This makes the broken bit difficult to see. I like white paint. It makes everything feel clean, and fixed. And it is cheap - and it dries really quickly.

LOVE
SICK

Gustav Meinhelm came to see me last year. He is quite serious, and unusual looking. At the time he was underweight and slept two or three hours a night. The bones stood out on his face. His eyes barely registered even strong light. And when he wept, he was unable to produce tears. He was lovesick. His lover had left him. He saw her face in everything. In you, me, in the shape of a cloud. He was slowly dying. But he didn't. I made him better. He left last week. I cannot sleep. Or eat. I am beside myself.

SUPERHERO

William Watts was the most sensible boy in our street. He was polite. He was good. My mother liked him a lot. He came to ours every Wednesday after school. One day William turned up wearing a Batman suit. Don't worry, he told us, everything's going to be okay. He picked up the kitchen table. He threw a pumpkin in the toilet. He did a press-up, kissed my mother and leapt out of the bathroom window. He punched the dog. He climbed the fence. He ran off down the street. That was the last time William Watts came to ours.

TOTAL ECLIPSE OF THE HEART

Martin Flowers was the greatest anthropologist the world has ever seen. Peter McGee was the second greatest anthropologist the world has ever seen. Peter wrote great books and discovered great things. Martin wrote greater books and discovered greater things. Peter wanted to be greater than Martin, so he decided to visit the heart eating Ybro tribe during a total eclipse. Don't go, said Martin. It's a total eclipse. They'll eat your heart. But Peter went and the Ybro ate his heart, just like Martin said they would. Martin's written a book about Peter's trip. It's brilliant. It's anthropology's greatest book.

CAFÉ UTOPIA

I am standing in my coffee shop. Everything is ready. There are ten tables. There are forty chairs. The walls are painted blue. The door is painted white. There is a real 1950s coffee machine. There are lots of cups. Each cup is different. It is much better that way. I have baked and iced the cakes. There is music playing. I have chosen all the CDs myself. I am looking around my coffee shop. The door is open. There is a block of light moving slowly across the floor. I am standing in my coffee shop. Everything is ready.

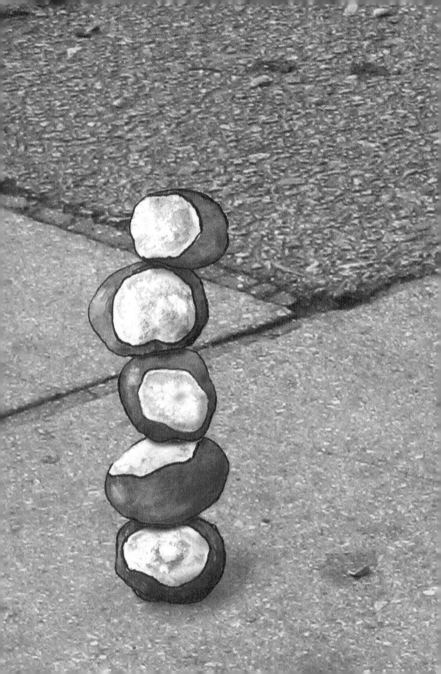

CONKERS

This morning I found some conkers. They were on the pavement on the way to town. Somebody must have put them there because there isn't a conker tree on that street. And they had taken special care about it too. Each conker was balanced, one on top of the other, in a kind of tower. It was quite beautiful, a tiny work of art. I don't know how long they had been there, or how they had survived without being kicked down. But as I looked at them, I felt really happy. I picked them up and took them home.

EXTRACT FROM THE DIARY OF A TOURIST

Michelangelo was an artist from Italy. Michelangelo's best work is a sculpture of a boy. The boy's name is David. David once killed a giant. He is a main character in a story called The Old Testament. The boy is naked. He is very good looking. He is twice as tall as a man. He looks real. He looks like he is about to turn from a stone boy into a real boy. Michelangelo called the sculpture *David*. I don't know why. If it was up to me, I would call it *David, The Handsome Boy*, or something like that.

SWEET CAROLINE

My girlfriend's name is Caroline. I met her in a bar. She's short. She has curly hair. She has a fast car. Come live with me, she said. So I did. She has a big house, a big swimming pool and a big garden. When I moved in, I had a job working for the bank. I did it for a bit, but then I stopped. Now I spend my time sunbathing and watching TV. Caroline says I should just lie about for the rest of my life. She brings me presents, and tickles my back. She is really nice.

A NEW HUSBAND

I have been married three times. The first was to a rich man. I am slightly ashamed to say I married him for his money. My second husband was a weightlifter. I met him on a beach. He had enormous thighs. My last husband was a farmer. He was long, beautiful. He had a blonde beard and way of walking that made me short of breath. He kept chickens, which he treated kindly. He let them into the house and upstairs and on the bed. I did not marry him for his chickens. I am looking for a new husband.

THE BINOCULARS BELONGING TO AMY WALTERS

My name is Sonkwe Akashambatwa. I am a lead guide at Victoria Falls. Last week Amy Walters disappeared. Amy was my client. I had taken her to Livingston Island (we have islands on the crest of the falls). It was just me and her. During the ride we talked a lot. She liked me. I told her I liked her binoculars. She asked that I leave her on the island. She said she wanted to be alone with the waterfall. When I returned, she was gone. I found the binoculars on a rock. I think Amy left them for me.

A THOUSAND THANK YOUS

One night in his sleep, Thomas Nightingale was visited by ghosts. They revealed to him the selfishness of his ways and offered a chance of redemption. To save his soul, Thomas was to find 1000 people to whom he owed a debt of thanks. He thanked his mother and he thanked his friends. He thanked his neighbours and his local newsagent. He thanked his old school teacher and all the players of his favourite football team. In short, Thomas did as he was told. He said thank you 1000 times. The ghosts went away. His soul is saved. The end.

I AM GOING TO FLY MY PLANE

This week I have been building a plane. I found the engine at a scrapyard. It is a Rolls Royce engine. My friend Jim gave me some wood and I am using three wheels from my car. Jim has fixed the controls. There is no seat. I am using my bathroom stool. Now the plane is ready. The engine is roaring. I am sitting on the stool. Lots of lights are flashing. I am so happy. In only one minute I am going to take off, fly over my house, fly over Jim's house, and then land back here. Goodbye.

HYAKUMO-NOGATARI KAIDANKAI

Hyakumonogatari Kaidankai is a game. It means A Gathering of 100 Supernatural Tales. It is played in a room of 100 candles. Each time a story is told, a candle is blown out. At the end, when the last candle is blown out, a god enters the room and special things happen. I only played it once. Some good stories were told. Lots of candles were blown out. I told the last story. I blew the candle out. The room went black. I got beaten up. I didn't see the god that did it. The others said it was massive.

THE MAP

Freddie Marchant built The Map. He was quite excited about it. He told us he had included the office and the pub and everybody's house. He told us we were all represented by a flashing light. One day I went round Freddie's house after the pub. He showed me The Map. He showed me flashing in his house. I was a red light. He showed me the pub and the rest of our friends. They were flashing too. They were green lights. I asked Freddie why I was the only red light. That's because I don't like you, he said.

ANGEL

This is a love story. A girl called Angel lived next door. There was something small wrong with her. She would run every day to swing in the park. I remember Angel's laugh. The way her hair turned red. How her legs caught the light. She let me do what I liked. Then I moved away. Then I got married. Then I left my wife. Other not so good things happened. I came home. The first person I saw was Angel. Her hair was grey. I said hello. She got off the swing. She kissed me. I took her home.

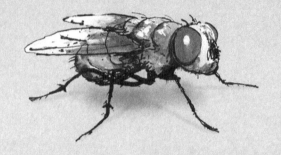

THE FACIST
AND THE FLY

At 7.33am Manuel Albinini leaves for work. Every morning I watch this man. His hair is slick, his moustache is trimmed and the shine on his shoes reflects his sanitary and disciplined life. Late at night, when the lights are on, I can see into his apartment, and into a world of white tiles and marble floors – all Wagner and disinfectant. Christ it makes my teeth ache. Anyway, yesterday, whilst he was out, I posted a live fly through his letterbox. This morning at 7.36 I watched Manuel Albinini leave for work, his top button undone and looking distinctly unshaven.

WHY BUNNY MASON DROWNED

Surviving a drowning means something. You have a second chance. You grab at life with both hands. At least this is the rule. There are exceptions: My friend Bunny Mason went for a ride along the beach last winter. This is a stupid thing to do. The waves there are like cliffs. People die doing this sort of thing. Anyway, Bunny did it. And was duly swept away. And then washed up, alive. She picked herself up and walked to the nearest petrol station. She bought a packet of ten cigarettes. Then Bunny went back to look for her bike.

AGRICULTURAL CUP

Timo Couper invented a board game. He called it Agricultural Cup. In Timo's game you had to buy all of the things that you need to run a really good farm. You had to buy seeds; then fertilisers; then you bought a chicken. Finally you got some cows, a tractor and a barn. The first person to buy all the things was the winner. Timo's game was not a success. Hardly anyone bought it. I remember hearing that Timo thought that this was because nobody's interested in farms. Not true. The game doesn't have any goats. Every farm has goats.

JUGS AND OTHER EUPHEMISMS

Whenever we go shopping, my flatmate and I play a simple game. We are only allowed to buy items that also mean a woman's breasts. You would be surprised at how many things this allows us to buy. We have bought jugs, yams, sponge cakes, spark plugs, earmuffs and bongos. However a typical basket often includes a couple of mangos, a juicy pear, two big melons, a lovely bunch of coconuts and some milkshakes. As you can see, this means we eat a whole lot of fruit. So I highly recommend this game, as it is both fun and healthy.

THE TREE

Margaret Leach decided to enter a poetry competition. She sat down and looked at her blank piece of paper. She sharpened her pencil. She made some tea. She played some inspirational music. Nothing happened, so she decided to go for a walk. The sun was shining and the birds were singing. It was a lovely day. She saw a beautiful tree and thought about the wind whispering through its leaves. Margaret's spirits were up. She went home and wrote her poem. She wrote it in five minutes. She called it The Tree. It was very good. It won first prize.

SQUEAK
PIGGY
SQUEAK

I shouldn't be telling you this. Last week I went to visit Sir
Roger McEnnan, the famous pig farmer. Roger is known for
having a way with pigs. When I arrived, Roger met me at the
gate with a whole bunch of them. They were very friendly. They
pushed against my legs, and sniffed my private parts, and one
licked my buttocks. At Roger's house, a lot of them came in and
lay about on the floor. After supper, Roger McEnnan said good
night. Then he and a pig went upstairs to bed, where they made
a lot of noise.

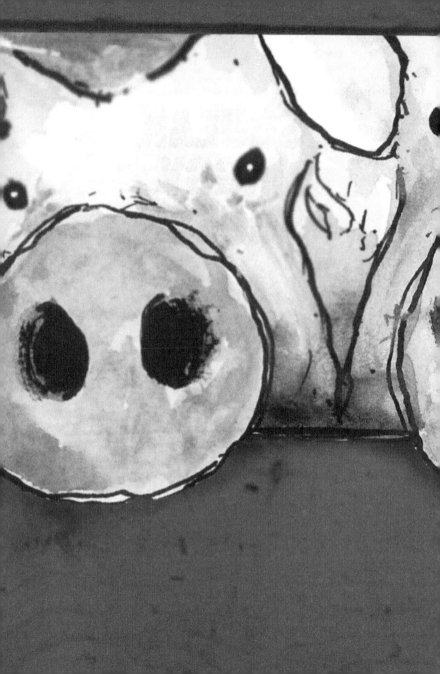

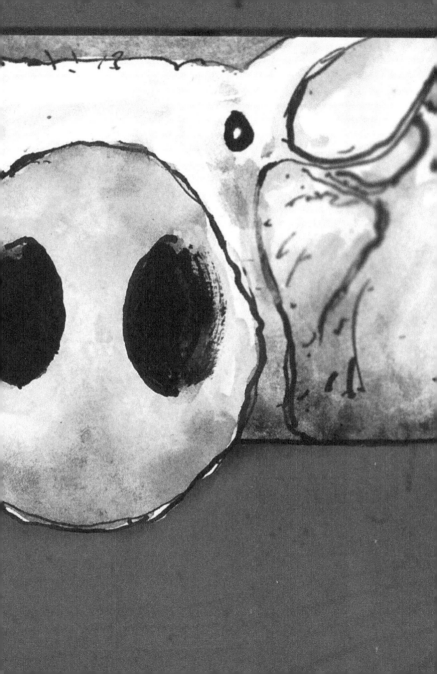

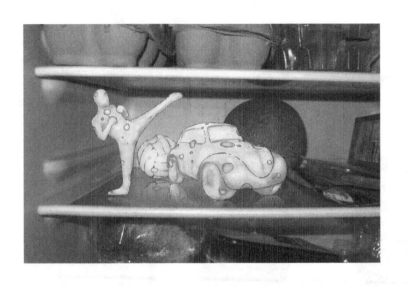

CHEESY LOVE

We met on the internet. He asked me what I liked. I said making things. I asked him what he liked. He said cars, football, kick boxing and cheese, in that order. That night, I got to work. From a large block of cheese I made a car, a football and a man doing a high kick. I put them in the fridge. We agreed to meet and I presented him with the things I had made. He laughed out loud. He said: Let's use them to make a pizza. That would be wonderful, I said. I love making things.

THE CURSE OF TUTANKHAMUN

Recently the cloth items, especially Tutankhamun's clothes, have been replicated in order to gain a better understanding of the King's body shape. This good idea was mine, and it seems that the wall art depicting the royal males with inordinately large hips is entirely accurate. Tutankhamun had a size 42 waist and looked like a pear. This reminds me of a remark in one of Howard Carter's journals: We all, when we come to Egypt, and work in the desert, lose a great deal of weight. This is untrue, for now it seems I cannot quite fit into my trousers.

RIVER DEEP, MOUNTAIN HIGH

Humbert Fieldman is a field volunteer at our National Park. He writes the signs. He has been doing this for nearly thirty years. He has written ENTRANCE and EXIT. He has written PLEASE MIND YOUR HEAD and DO NOT FEED THE BEARS. Every sign he writes is a masterpiece. Recently Humbert told me that he wanted to write a sign for everything in the park. He seems to be working faster than ever. I have counted seventy-four BIG TREEs and ninety-eight SMALL ROCKs. There is even a RIVER DEEP, MOUNTAIN HIGH. I have asked someone to tell Humbert to stop.

THE PAMPAS GRASS OF ETERNAL HAPPINESS

It is written that everything is a symbol. I am not sure about this. In my street there lives a man called Hercules Mollato. He is always in his front garden, tending a great bushel of pampas grass. Some say that pampas grass is a sign of promiscuity. I am not sure about this, but it is well known that Hercules and Maria Mollato live behind their curtains, and that they entertain frequently. My wife believes they will come to no good. I am not sure about this. I saw Hercules yesterday afternoon, with his pampas grass. He looked happy.

BRASSO

I am a clean person. I like to be clean and I like to clean things. I like soap. I like detergent. And I like Brasso. Brasso is brilliant. Brasso is the best cleaning product ever. I have had it for a week. I have used it on knives and forks, on taps and lots of other metal stuff. My home smells nice, and it is shiny. Yesterday, I used it on a dirty apple. I ate the apple. It tasted good. Afterwards, I noted that my teeth were whiter. Then I lay down for a bit. Brasso is great.

MODERN ROMANCE

Chris and I went to the same school. He was obsessed with the 21st century. He used to tell me about the things we would have when we grew up - floating cars, laser guns, a penis that was also a vagina. Anyway, Chris moved away soon after we left school. Ten years went by. Then Chris asked to be my friend on Facebook. I said yes. We chatted a lot. He invited me to his house. I went. He did not have a floating car or a laser gun. But he did have a brand new vagina. So I stayed.

ANIMAL, VEGETABLE, MINERAL

Animal, Vegetable, Mineral is a diet book, written by Doctor Karl Cooper. Doctor Karl's promise is simple: eat one portion of animal, one portion of vegetable and one portion of mineral rich food for every meal, and your life will change. He is a handsome and successful man. He has an impressive beard. He is often on telly. He says that everything about him is a result of his diet. I bought myself Doctor Karl's book. I rigorously followed his plan. But it has only partially worked. I am still not handsome or successful. But my beard is very impressive.

Before...

After...

TWENTY QUESTIONS

Whenever I meet someone new, I always ask them twenty questions. I tell them it is a game. But really it isn't: I am finding out quickly what they are like. I start by asking their name. This leaves me nineteen more questions. Then I ask them where they come from, and about their religion and their politics. Some of the questions I ask are choices – Disco or Punk? Cats or Dogs? Questions like this can tell you a lot about someone. But it is always the last question that is the most important. Do you like me? I say.

CAT MAN

Toni Jarrad is well known around here. He keeps to himself. He loves cats. He works at the pet shop, and three times a week he plays football for us. He's good. I've always had a lot of time for Toni Jarred. Not anymore. It's like this: The place we play is borrowed, and we lock up. Last Friday was Toni's turn. We all live close, and I'd forgotten my boots. I went back. The door was open. I went in. Toni was in the middle of the hall, licking his arse. Toni Jarred is not in the team anymore.

BANKER

My friend Thomas Henderson is a top banker. And he is handsome. And he has everything. Earlier this year, Thomas was watching the news. It was about some people starving to death somewhere in Africa. The next day he began a fast. He said it was in the name of all starving Africans. We decided to bet on how long he would last. The bets grew very large. Thomas got wind of the sweepstake. He called me and a couple of other close friends. He told us exactly when the fast would end. And we made a lot of money.

THE CYCLIST

Some stories are about nothing at all. This is one of them. Paul Regan and I work in the same office. On occasion we share a desk. Once we did a job together. Paul is a cyclist. During work hours you would be hard pushed to tell the difference between us, but afterwards Paul cycles home. At the weekend he cycles around the countryside and during the holidays he...Well, you get the picture. I think he will cycle all the way to his grave. I have known Paul for twenty years. I have never spoken to him about cycling.

THE BARISTA

Emilio Rodriguez worked in a coffee shop near me. He was the best barista I have ever known. It wasn't just the taste of his coffee. It was how it looked. He could draw anything in the froth on top. I loved watching Emilio. He was stylish and quick. We all tried to think of harder and harder things for him to draw - a wildebeest, an angle poise lamp, a TV with someone on it - but there was no beating him. Then one day Emilio told us that he had a problem with his passport. We haven't seen him since.

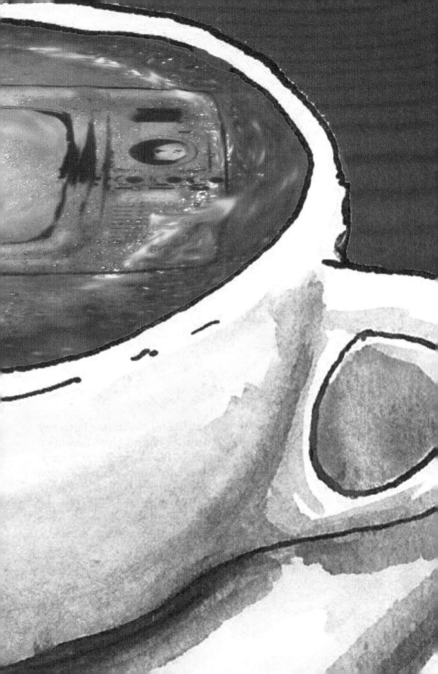

JOHN'S IN CHARGE

I am giving everything up to John Hazel. John has been my assistant for almost ten years. In that time I have become a world famous photographer. I am rich. I have a beautiful family. I travel the world. Much of this is down to John. John has always been there, by my side. He knows the camera better than I do. He understands the computer. My diary is his diary. He made me. Now he says he wants everything - house, my career and even the family. I've said yes. So has my wife. And the children. John's in charge.

I HAD
A FRIEND

I had a friend. Her name was Alicia Sandcliff. At school Alicia was known for not doing the right thing. She left school. She hung about with us. She started to drink. She got a job with the council. She drank some more. She lost her job. Then she got hit on the head by a car. It affected her. She stopped hanging about with us. She rented a flat. She decorated the flat. She got a new job. She met someone. Now she's pregnant. She's not my friend anymore. I wish a car would hit me on the head.

SOME PEOPLE HAVE ALL THE LUCK

Frank Jenner was beautiful. He and I went to the same drama school, and occasionally, in the early days, we got drunk together. Then Frank got lucky. A soup company whose name we all know used him to sell their cans. He was a hit, and Frank went off the radar. I saw him everywhere – billboards, television, in magazines. One day Frank died while filming a commercial. A stunt involving a pallet of soup cans (I am not making this up) went wrong. I went to the funeral. And then I got a really good job, better even than Frank's.

YOU'LL NEVER WALK ALONE

Chicory Smith has fallen in love with a girl. She has brown hair and beautiful eyes. She catches the same bus as him in the mornings. She works in the same building. Chicory has been watching the girl. She is never with anyone. When he sees her at lunch or on her way home she is always by herself. He thinks she is sad. He wants to help her. He wants to do something romantic. He buys her some flowers and a card. In it he writes: You'll never walk alone. He leaves it with the flowers on her desk.

FAMILY

We've had Dad's wake. It was good for a bit. It made me think of lots of things. His accordion. The bread he ate. His lap. The smell of his cheek. Mum was there. And Charlie. And Auntie Pat. It felt good and we all had a group hug and a bit of a cry. Everyone was dressed to the nines. There was tea and cake and sherry and I felt happy. But then Charlie had a go at me for eating all the biscuits. Mum gave me a slap. People left. And that was the end of Dad's wake.

GORILLA

I am a gorilla. I am intelligent and family-orientated and strong. My back is beginning to turn silver. My coat is warm. My teeth are large. I beat my chest whenever I feel like it. I am a strict vegetarian. I like mountains. I try not to climb a tree. I can smell the possibility of sex long before it appears. Keep me in a cage and I will forget myself. I don't mind you looking at me. I don't mind you being around me. I do mind you talking to me. Do not touch me. I am a gorilla.

POOR OLIVER HOUSEN

Oliver Housen was a good man. He looked you in the eyes. He spoke gently. He ran a local charity. The charity specialised in recovering alcoholics. It had a high success rate. Then one Christmas Oliver disappeared. The charity floundered and the streets were once again filled with people drinking low-grade alcohol. A year later, when jogging beside the river, I sat down next to a man drinking beer from an old water bottle. It was Oliver Housen. I couldn't believe my eyes. Poor Oliver Housen. He looked terrible. Oliver, I said, you look terrible. Fuck off, he said, gently.

FREE
BEER

Last week, I read about a man who drove around the country giving away free ice creams. He said it made him happy. I thought this was a brilliant idea. I bought an old blue van and filled it with beers. I drove down to the beach and gave away the beer. The people at the beach loved it and kept coming back for more. It made me really happy to give them more and more beers. Then the beer ran out and the people went away. I sat in the back of the van. It was big and empty.

A SMALL ACT OF REBELLION

The supermarket where I shop has a car park. The car park is underneath the supermarket. In order to get from the car park to the supermarket you have to take an escalator. Whenever you are travelling on the escalator you always hear a loud voice. The loud voice tells you to be careful. It always says the same thing. It says: Please hold the handrail whilst travelling. Whenever I am travelling on the escalator I make a point of not holding the handrail. Sometimes, when I am travelling down the escalator, I hold my hands high in the air.

PROGRESS

In 1976 Constance Everly treated herself to a brand new shopping trolley. It had a strong frame, a plastic handle and a nice green tartan basket - perfect for Constance's tins of shortbread biscuits. She never looked back. But not forward either, and while we all bought cars and raced each other to the supermarket, Constance continued her battle along the pavement to the corner shop. In 2006 Constance Everly bent down to retrieve a Bakewell Tart that had slipped through a tear in the green tartan basket. She was struck squarely on the head by a van delivering online groceries.

A VICTORIAN
GENTLEMAN

A change had come over Leslie Boyle. He had taken to the classics in pursuit of a reading group, an interest and some friends. But then came the large moustache, the cape and the cane, which he tapped whilst standing beneath streetlights – the damp mists gathering around him. Billowing in silhouette, he would stride to the library, Dickens and Doyle clutched to his breast. And so it went on, billowing, swooping and striding. And lurking and lurking - and lurking. Until finally they noticed him, and threw their beer cans at him, and called him a wanker. So he went home.

MY BEAUTIFUL WIFE

Sylvia Brown, business woman and lover. Long blonde hair and a perfect back. She gets out of bed and pulls back the curtains. Light splashes through the house. Clean teeth and patent heels and a briefcase crammed with papers. There is the sound of water and of beautiful eating. I close my eyes and watch her gently sipping tea. I hear the door go. I get up. The air is cold but her smell lingers and I breathe it in. There is lipstick on the cup. My wife has gone to work. I love her. I will miss her terribly.

TRISTAN DI STEFANO HAS A FLAT AT THE TOP OF MY BUILDING

Tristan di Stefano has a flat at the top of my building. I often meet him in the lift. He is always dressed well, and carries a cane. Tristan tells me stories. They are about his villas, his ex-wives, his mistresses, his yachts and cars and private planes. Tristan's stories are boring and I don't believe them. So yesterday, after he told me about winning a lot of cash at the casino, I told Tristan that I was in trouble, and that I needed a thousand pounds. He gave me the money. Something to be getting on with, he said.

BEARDS

I am a big fan of beards. I have one for every occasion. I have a driving beard. It helps me change gear without looking. I have a beard for drinking beer. It is especially short around the mouth. I have a beard for kissing people. It makes my lips look fat and red. I have a beard for going to the toilet. It is long and much better than toilet paper. When I masturbate, I wear a stiff spade shaped beard. It is perfect for scooping the blobs of semen off my stomach. I have so many good beards.

NICE
MAN

Yesterday I had to take a train. The train was very busy. A man came and sat down next to me. He was wearing a suit. He was listening to music. He read an electronic book. He got out his laptop and went online. Then he made a phone call. He was on his phone for a long time. During the conversation he didn't say much. Then he got up and left all his stuff and he still hadn't come back when I reached my stop. I looked at his laptop. I thought about taking it. But then I didn't.

I AM
HAPPY

My name is Archibald Brindle. I like golf and I like fishing. I like discos and I like cats. I like eating Spanish food and drinking heavy wines. I like the sound of the seagulls in the morning and I like the sunshine on my face as I walk through the park. I have a boyfriend and a girlfriend and colourful shirts that make people smile. Life is a gift and everything is a wonder to behold. I really am full up to the brim. I can't stand to see an unhappy face. People like that need a good slap.

SHIP
OF FOOLS

Kristian Smiley, an estate agent with too many fast cars. Maurice Goldsworthy, his job in the city and his camel hair coat. Barnaby Guiness, all cigars and stubbly kisses. Hannah Foster with her skirt far too short. And the others, I knew them all. All friends since school. And then they went off in Barnaby's boat, with a bucket full of fireworks and a crate of champagne - terrorizing the estuary the whole afternoon. Until it was time for the fireworks. It was an intense if brief display. What else can I say? They were fools, every single one of them.

SHOUTING LOUDLY

Kingston B Rottam is a forty-five year old white man. He lives in London. He is very loud. From the moment he gets up, to the moment he goes to sleep, all he does is shout. He shouts at his wife, and he shouts at his children. At work he shouts at his employees. However, he reserves his absolute ire for public servants, at whom he screams until his voice packs up; until his mouth has emptied itself of spit; until his eyes turn red. As a result, you will always find Mr Rottam at the front of the queue.

BELGIAN BEER

There is something wonderful about Belgian beer. Originally monks brewed it, and drank it themselves. Now it is available to all of us. It comes in many sizes, and many colours, but the type I like fits comfortably in my drinking hand. It is light and golden, and when I drink it I think of the sun. I drink it everywhere I go. I drink bottle after bottle, and I never get drunk. It makes me feel strong, like a boxer, or a hundred metres runner. Sometimes, when I am alone, I practice jumping high. The Belgians are excellent people.

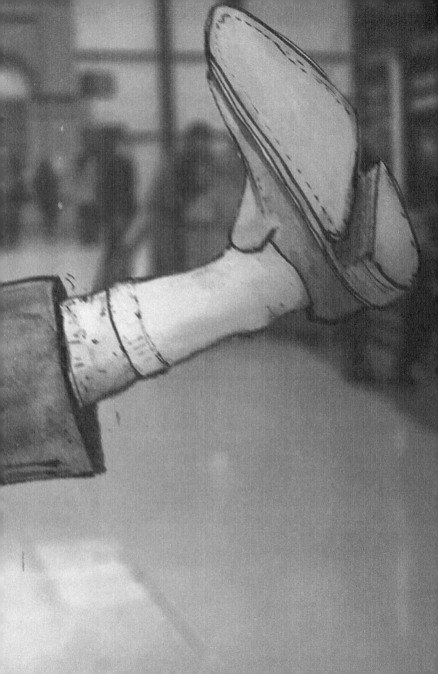

THE
NOTE

Archie Hunter was my friend. He carried around this folded bit of paper. He called it The Note. He said it helped him. One day I took Archie's note off him. He did a karate kick. He fell over. I gave Archie back The Note. He was okay. Then Archie moved away. The next time I saw him we were all grown up. I asked him about The Note. He opened his fist. It was The Note. I said, No way, and took it off him. He did a karate kick. He fell over. I gave Archie back The Note.

NOW THAT I HAVE A TABLET COMPUTER

Now that I have a tablet computer I can do anything. It is slim and silver and very light. It fits in my briefcase. Most of the time I don't know I have it. At home I keep it on the bottom shelf, next to the books. When I meet my friends for a coffee, I just put it to the side, out of the way, and have a good conversation. Also, if I am nowhere near a mirror, all I have to do is look in the screen. Everything is much better now that I have a tablet computer.

STEVEN'S HOUSE

Steven Foster lives near me. Steven has the same kind of house as me. We both live alone. We share the same taste in clothes. We like the same food. Our walls are green. We used to laugh about this. It made us happy. Once I gave Steven a hug. I told him that I loved his house very much. He said he loved my house too. We became great friends. One day we measured all the rooms, which is how we found out that Steven's front room is a foot wider than mine. I don't know what to do.

THE GROUPIES

I first met Martha Jackson at a local painting group. She was nice and we started going out together. I found out that Martha liked meeting people and learning new things; and that she loved joining new groups. We started joining groups together. We joined a car maintenance group and Alcoholics Anonymous. Then something horrible happened. Martha suggested we join a group called White is Right. So we did. You had to wear a white hood, go on marches and set fire to things. I no longer see Martha. I had to stop going. The hood made my face itch.

MY
BIG HAND

I have a big hand. The first thing people notice about me is my big hand. I don't mind. There are many advantages to having a big hand. It is very good at waving. It has an exceptional grip. It can hold a lot. Many children like to high five my big hand. It is a useful hand. It is also strong. I can squeeze an apple with it. My girlfriend loves my big hand. I shouldn't really say this, but it comfortably spans her above average sized buttocks. This makes her happy. I am a physically advantaged young man.

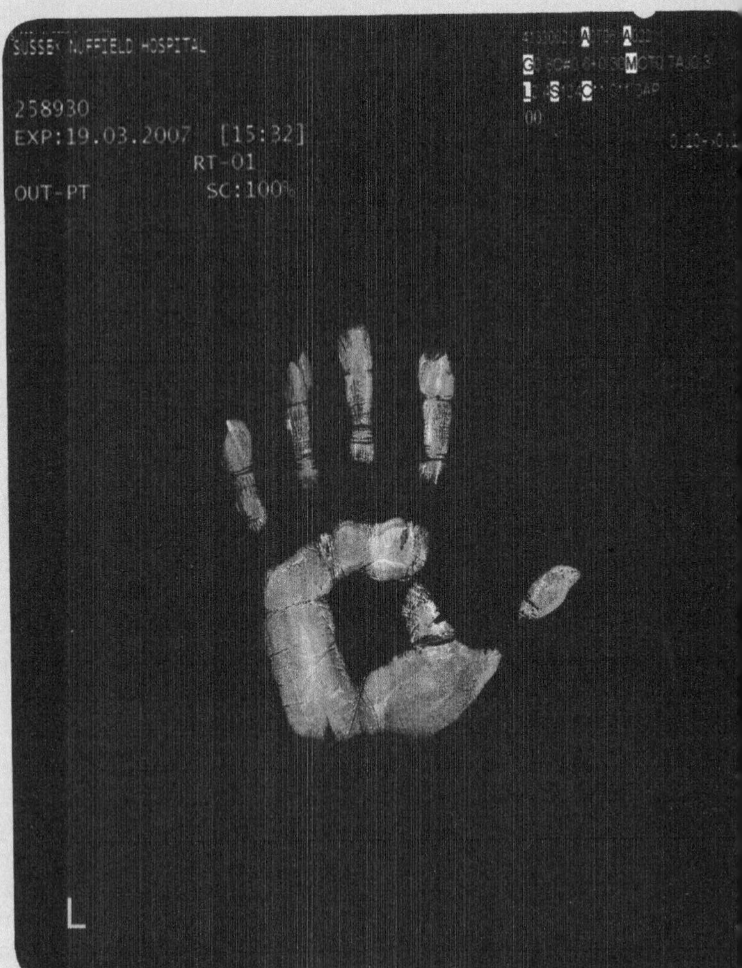
SUSSEX NUFFIELD HOSPITAL
258930
EXP:19.03.2007 [15:32]
RT-01
OUT-PT
SC:100%
L

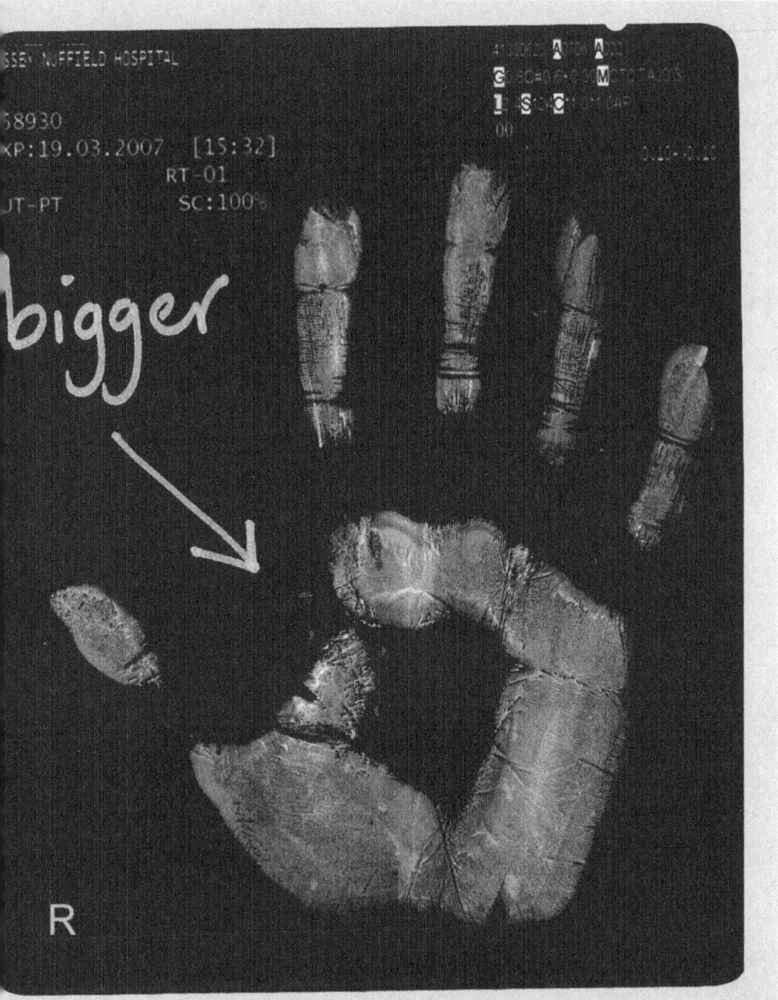

SSEX NUFFIELD HOSPITAL
58930
XP:19.03.2007 [15:32]
RT-01
JT-PT
SC:100%
bigger
R

A glass half full

by Gregor Krompton

No 1
Bestseller

A GLASS
HALF FULL

Gregor Krompton was a glass half full kind of guy. Literally. Whenever we went to the pub together he would order half a pint of beer in a pint glass. If we met for coffee he would insist on drinking espressos out of large mugs. I often pointed out to Gregor that this was a fairly futile exercise. But he just laughed and told me it was important to visualise concrete examples of positive thinking. Eventually Gregor put his ideas into a self-help book. A lot of the pages were blank. He was delighted with it. It sold quite well.

COLOURED STICKERS

Last week I lost my job. I had to clear out my desk. I put everything into a box and took it home. Amongst the pens and paper clips were several packs of Post-It notes. They were completely unused. Later that day I got bored. I decided to write a fact on each note. I stuck all the facts on my wall. I wanted to see how many things I knew. I used nearly three whole packs of post-it notes. Now the walls of my flat are covered in coloured stickers. It really is quite impressive how much I know.

NID BLYTON
aloud.

ALWAYS blames
his tools.

Aspidistr
need very
water

GLAND played
WHAM HOTSPUR
ALES

The Tropic of Cancer
is in the NORTHEEN
HEMISPHERE

Dettol kil
of all kno
bacteri

rk is NOT

Indian Elephants
have SMALL ears.

SUZIE GI

MY MOST FAVOURITE PEN

When I was little I put my favourite pen in my anus. I tried to get it out with some tweezers, which is how my mother found out. I went to hospital. They took an X-ray. The pen had moved further up inside me. The doctors said it would come out within two to three days. It did not. Other things happened. I grew up. I got married. I had kids. My mother died. Then yesterday I went to the toilet. I passed something long and hard. It was my favourite pen. I've given it a wash. It still works.

LIVING IN
LA VIDA LOCA

La Vida Loca is my hometown. It has a mayor and some streets and shops and a library and lots of bars. During the day it is dusty and during the night it is dangerous. Everyone has a gun. An armed guard rides the school bus. And some vultures live in the cliffs behind my house. There are no jobs here. Most of us are on drugs. My father's on drugs. I have only ever left La Vida Loca one time, when I went to the city to visit a friend. It was the most boring week of my life.

THE CACTUS

Weoboly Fields brought his cactus to work. Whenever you saw him, you couldn't help but notice his cactus. He even took it to meetings. This is odd, but no one said anything. The other day we all went for a drink. Weoboly placed his cactus on the bar and told us some stuff about it being him and about how his fate was wrapped up in the well being of the cactus. We all laughed. Weoboly hasn't been at work for a week. His cactus is still on his desk. It looks kind of brown. I wonder if it's dead.

I HAVE
A PARROT

I have a parrot. I show my parrot films. It likes black and white films. It likes Humphrey Bogart. It likes a film called The Maltese Falcon. It says lines from The Maltese Falcon. It has a favourite line. It says, When you're slapped, you'll take it and like it. It says this when I get up, when I leave, come home and when I go to bed. It says it in the middle of the night. I tell my parrot to stop it. My parrot does not stop it. I slap my parrot. It takes it. It likes it.

THE
BEN STORY

I know a man called Ben. When Ben is talking he likes to prefix the things he is talking about with his name. For example: Ben lives in the Benhouse. He drives the Bencar. In his bengarden he has benbeques and serves beer from the Benbar. Sometimes he gets completely benfucked and forgets how to benspeak. Ben has two benbinos, Ben Junior and Benjimina, and Mrs Ben is a very beautiful woman. Friday next week is the benbirthday. I have found out that there is a football team called Benfica. I have bought him their kit. He will love it.

MY BROTHER THE PAINTER

My brother can't speak. That's why he paints. When he was a boy, he painted boys. When he was a teenager, he painted girls. When Dad left Mum, he painted Dad. My brother's painted us hundreds of times. He used to paint us in different places – in the garden, on holiday, in the street. Sometimes he painted us with our friends, our relatives and our neighbours. But now Mum's dead, he just paints me. I visit my brother once a month. He lives at the top of a large house. I climb the stairs. He paints me. Then I go.

SUNGLASSES

Sunglasses are the best things ever. I have worn them all my life. I like all types of sunglasses but my favourites are the ones worn by pilots. I wear pilot sunglasses whenever I want to do things quickly. Pilots have very fast reactions. They think fast. I like to wash up in pilot sunglasses. My second most favourite sunglasses are ones that make the world look yellow. I like looking at trees, houses, cars and faces through them. My third most favourite sunglasses are really big ones. They make me feel clever. I am wearing a pair right now.

FLYING SAUCER

I have seen a flying saucer. It was dark when I saw it. It lit up the sky. I told all my friends. They just laughed at me. Then Martha Jones got to hear about it. Martha Jones is not my friend. She kept asking me questions about it. It was dark I told her, it lit up the sky. Martha did not laugh. She gave me magazines. She printed pictures off the internet. She would not go away. Martha said that she wished she had seen the flying saucer. I wish I hadn't, I said. She didn't believe me.

FRED B. ONCE TURNED UP

Fred B. once turned up at the office with a bandage wrapped around his head. He said his gas cooker was faulty and left it at that. Later I found out what really happened. Unbeknown to us, Fred enjoyed lighting his hair, putting it out and smelling the palms of his hands. But then something had gone wrong. We found this funny. We began to light our hair at work - to see how Fred would react. After a while, Fred left the company. We stopped lighting our hair, which is a pity because I liked the smell of it.

SQUIRRELED

Yesterday, a squirrel followed Godfrey McDonald home. Godfrey lives close to a park, which has both trees and squirrels. Sometimes Godfrey goes to the park to stretch his legs. Which is what he did yesterday, before the squirrel followed him home. It followed him out of the park, across the road and up the street. It followed him to his front door. Godfrey closed the door before the squirrel could get in. He forgot about the squirrel and got on with the rest of his day. But this morning, when Godfrey opened his front door, the squirrel was still there.

A BAD THING IS ABOUT TO HAPPEN

My name is Joseph Abendigo Sawyer. It is. I am God fearing. I go to church. I kneel. People know me. I am upstanding. I can preach. My house is simple. I work hard. When I walk, I walk with God. I have never seen the sea, the inside of an aeroplane, a really big tree. The land here is very red. There are rocks. Snakes. Ants. The sky is empty, the nights are cold. It has been this way forever. I am forty-four years old. I have no family. Some days I forget how to speak. I really do.

INGEL
INGELTON

Ingel Ingelton had it all: a good business, a good wife, a firm belief in the love of God. He loved us and we loved him. But no man is just happy. Ingel Ingelton also had an unfortunate obsession with the right arm of Eva Grön. I once saw Eva's arm. It was a normal arm, ageing, long and always on the move. Eva worked for Ingel and was required to wear very short sleeves. Time passed and now Eva's arm has been found in Ingel's freezer. I am open-mouthed. Ingel Ingelton is not the man I thought he was.

MY ELECTRIC BAR HEATER

I don't have a fireplace in my house. I have an electric bar heater. It is a portable electric bar heater, and it has a long lead, which means I can warm up any room, even the toilet. I love my bar heater. I like to light my cigarette on the bars. I am an adult, and I don't have children of my own, so I've removed the heater's protective frame. I use it to dry my clothes, and sometimes my hair. When I've got nothing to do, I switch it on. It is the centre point of my home.

TIDDLY WINKS

Ginger Spellman is a friend of mine. He is very good at tiddly winks. He has won lots of competitions. He is always practicing. Whenever I meet Ginger for a drink after work, he amuses himself by landing counters in my beer; or on top of my head. Once he even managed to get seven tiddly winks to stick to the side of my face. Ginger is a special player. Sometimes, after an evening of the most amazing tricks, I will look him straight in the eye and say: Ginger, you are the best tiddly winker ever. You really are.

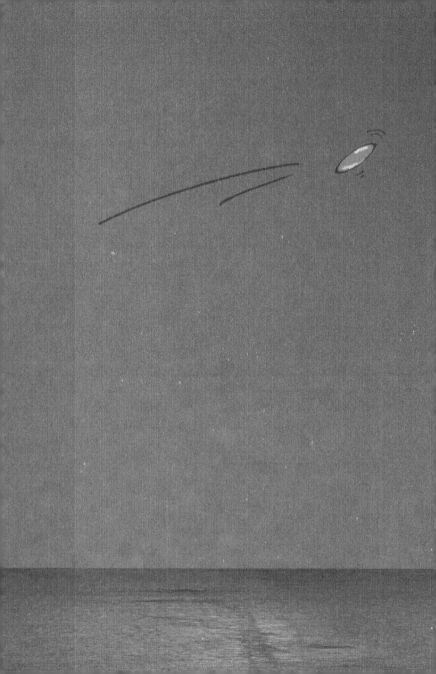

THIS SPORTING LIFE

When I was a boy my father tried his very best to get me to play sports. We went to the park every Saturday. He would throw me a ball. I would drop the ball. My father never showed his disappointment. He just smiled and said, Don't worry. It will come. But it didn't. I was no good. I had no sporting ability. I couldn't catch. Then my father got sick. He was dying. On the last day of his life, he sat up in bed. He threw me something. It was an orange. I caught it with both hands.

MY FRIEND CARDINAL RICHELIEU

My friend Robert Galesworth has started pretending he is Cardinal Richelieu. He has a long robe and a red skull cap. He has grown a beard. Yesterday, things got out of hand. Robert started asking people if they were Protestant or Catholic. If they answered Catholic, then he held their face in his hands and gently kissed them on the forehead. If they answered Protestant, then he tutted loudly and turned away. I asked Robert why he did this. He said it was because Protestants don't believe in transubstantiation. Then he smiled and walked slowly away, mumbling in old French.

WHERE THE FUCK ARE MY POTS?

I am a potter. I make pots. I have my own shop. My shelves are full of my pots. People come in and buy them. Those that know say I have my own style. A lot of my friends have been to my shop. They always buy my pots. When I go to my friends' for dinner or a barbeque, I make a point of checking through their cupboards. There is always a lot of beautiful crockery - my friends have fantastic taste. I love looking at their stuff. But there is always something missing. Where the fuck are my pots?

YESTERDAY I WENT TO THE BEACH

Yesterday I went to the beach. I had the sand all to myself. I found a hollow in the dunes and closed my eyes. I must have slept a little time because when I sat up I saw I had been joined by a man and a woman. The woman sat in a deckchair with her back to the wind whilst the man set about launching a number of kites. Each time he tethered the kite to a stick and drove it into the sand. I counted at least fifty kites. I have no idea what to make of this.

MOB
RULE

Life is confusing. Take, for example, Maria and Santos Peredes, sister and brother, whose desire for one another was a lifelong habit. Agreeing never to have children, Maria and Santos lived together without shame. Like any couple, they argued, but we may surmise that their lovemaking was both artless and knowing. We all know this is wrong. I should like to say that I knew nothing; that Maria took in my laundry; and that Santos and I worked together at Brenkinter's on South Street. The truth is: I knew, and will throw the first rock to prove I did not.

HAYDEN'S NEW HAIRCUT

I have known Hayden Lewes for a very long time. And in that time he has (until very recently, which is why I am writing about it) always had the same haircut. It was longish and neglected looking. I thought it went with his personality, which has always been charmingly passive. But then last week Hayden got himself a new haircut. It is closely cropped. It looks darker. It makes his face look bigger. His neck is bare. I am almost embarrassed by the sight of Hayden's bare neck. It is long and pale and I want to touch it.

JUST
SAY NO

Last year Leonardo Van Vier decided he was tired of saying yes. All these undiscovered opportunities suddenly didn't have any meaning anymore. He was himself and he was where he was and no longer was anyone going to distract him from it. There were many things Leonardo did not want to do and so whenever an option presented itself, he would decline politely and gracefully, glad of no longer having to decide whether this was indeed an opportunity worth having. Exciting. Liberating. Reductive. Leonardo is now living alone, in his room, without so much as a tinker's worth of hope.

THE GATE GAME

When I was at school, we played a game called The Gate. It was an easy game. Someone would shout, The Gate - and we would make a gate out of our bodies. Somebody would be the frame. Somebody would be the handle. Somebody would be a stop. Somebody would be the actual gate. Then we would stay there, and wait for someone to come. If someone did come, we would try to get them to go through us. If somebody didn't come, we would stay there for a few minutes – about five minutes – and then stop playing. It was fun.

FEMME FATALE

She had big red lips and long blonde hair. When I ran over her cat, she invited me in. She asked me to sit down. She brought me a drink. We smoked cigarettes and she told me about her cat. It was scratchy, she said. It was never home. I looked at her lips. I looked at her hair. She touched my knee. She did not smile. As I was leaving, a dog barked. It's my husband's, she said. She leaned forward and kissed my cheek. Tomorrow, she said. I picked up a stick and threw it into the road.

AN ISOLATED COMMUNITY

We should have seen it coming. When a man like Smarly Maltid moves to a house in the woods and starts making leather lampshades to swap for food, it is not the stuff of happy endings. At first nobody really noticed the disappearances. After all, people come and go. Then, when her husband failed to return home, Mrs Anderson discovered several of his tattoos adorning the lamp that Smarly had just traded for one of her pies. The shock was universal, and bad things happened to Smarly Maltid. But Mrs Anderson kept the lamp for reading. We are practical people.

POINTS

Opinions are a waste of time. I have a much better system. I give everything points out of 10. Here's how it works. I give my house 8 out of 10. My car is a 9. My girlfriend is a 6 out of 10. She was a 7 but now she's 6. My mum's a 7. She is better than my girlfriend but not as good as the house. Playstation just gets 6, Xbox a 9 and walking in the countryside a 2. I give my current haircut an 8, the summer a 5, and my dog, Rupert, a 10.

ARTISTS

Sarah Suleman was a normal person. Except she died young; and had a picture of herself for every day between January 1st, 1999 and September 11th, 2008. Each picture was taken at the same time, in the same place. There is no background – just Sarah's face, which never smiles. This record of my friend was displayed on a wall in her flat. She said it helped her remember. When she got sick she made me promise to take a photograph of her dead face. I did. Out of all the pictures of Sarah, it is by far my absolute favourite.

TOP
SPIN

I play tennis. My favourite shot is the top spin shot. It is a
beautiful shot. I practise it at home. I practise it in front of
the mirror. I practise it in the bath. I practise it when I am
buttering my toast. I have incorporated it into everything I do.
Some parts of my body are very good at the top spin shot. My
tongue is very good at playing the shot. I like to practise with
it on soft boiled eggs. I like to do it all the time. My wife doesn't
mind. It's a top shot.

THE BOTHERSOME CUSTOMER

I have a favourite café. I go there a lot. I have a favourite table. It is near the electricity point. This is where I plug my laptop in. I really like the café's lattes. They serve them in mugs. A latte costs two pounds. The café has its own wireless network. This means I can sit in the café for hours and hours and do things on my laptop. I always leave a tip at the end of the day. I always say Bye and See you tomorrow, but the staff at the café are too busy to answer.

A WORD IN YOUR SHELL LIKE

Jonathan Jones covered his house with shells. He went to the beach and found each one himself. Then he took it home and set it in a tiny square of concrete. He did this every weekend until it was finished. It took him a very long time. When it was sunny, people came and looked at the house. They pointed and took photographs. When this happened, Mrs. Jones would stay inside trying to keep away from the windows. But Jonathan ran straight down the garden path. 'Ere, a word in your shell like, he would say. And everyone would laugh.

CLEAN
HAIR

Some people say that we are shaped by our childhood experiences. I do not subscribe to this theory. When I was young my mother was obsessed with my hair. Each night she would stand me on a chair in only my underpants. She put on a pair of washing up gloves. She hit my head with a roll of newspaper. She scrubbed my hair with hand soap. Then she sent me to bed with a plastic bag taped to my head. She did this every night. My mother was quite mad. But I am fine. And I have clean hair.

VOODOO HOODOO

Yesterday was my birthday. My friends came round and they gave me presents. One of the presents was a real voodoo doll. Michael Brooks was also there. He did not bring me a present. When my friends had gone I drew Michael's face on the doll and twisted its arms hard. Then the bell went. It was Michael. He had forgotten his keys. I gave Michael his keys and watched him go. He walked for a bit. Then he skipped and swung his arms about happily in the air. I stopped watching Michael. I threw the doll in the bin.

THE PENIS GAME

When I was at school, we played a game called The Penis Game. It was a simple game. It began when one weekend I managed to slip a marble into my foreskin. I showed my friends on Monday, at break. Everyone was impressed. We spent the rest of the week practising with the class marbles. It became our favourite game. More and more people started doing it. We held a competition. We called it The Penis Game Competition. The whole school entered. A boy was caught with 8 marbles in his penis. The Penis Game was banned. In assembly. Forever.

THE TIME I MET AN EXCITING CUSTOMER

Some time ago a man called Justin Fuller booked my boat. He turned up in a wheelchair. He had no legs and only one arm. He said he wanted to see the biggest shark I could find. He had a lot of money. We went straight out. I baited the water. He looked at the water. I smoked a cigarette. Then the bait got hit, and Mr Fuller's arm began to shake. He tried to speak. He closed his eyes. He told me that he had lost his limbs to a shark in three separate incidents. Three? I said, excitedly.

THE STAKEOUT

Dell Harvey paid me to follow his wife. I followed his wife. She did lots of things. I took photographs. I did not see her with another man. I lived in my car. I ate in my car. I grew a beard. I drank beer. I continued to take photographs. I photographed everything I saw. Eventually my camera ran out of batteries. This afternoon I smoked some cigarettes and took a nap. When I woke up I drank a bottle of whisky. I saw Mrs Harvey. She was with a man. I can't say for sure if it wasn't Dell.

SPIDER FIGHT

A favourite children's pastime is spider fighting. What you do is find two spiders, put them in a bowl and watch them fight. Sometimes the spiders will not fight. Sometimes they prefer to copulate. And sometimes the little one will let the big one eat it. Most spiders like to fight in September, and in May, after a winter break. The best fighting spider is a brown spider. Spider fighting has many benefits – too many to mention here – and is popular throughout the world, except in Antarctica, the Arctic, Greenland, Iceland and some small islands whose names I have forgotten.

THE DOOR

I have a friend called Paul Hendricks. Paul is an architect. He designs concrete houses. He is very successful. Paul's most successful design is called The Door. It is called The Door because it only has one door. It has a front door. He lives in one. Paul likes to invite his friends round, where he talks a lot about the virtues of one-door living. I went once, but I am not very successful. I live in a flat. It has 8 doors. So I got angry at Paul and left - through the window, which was clever. I think.

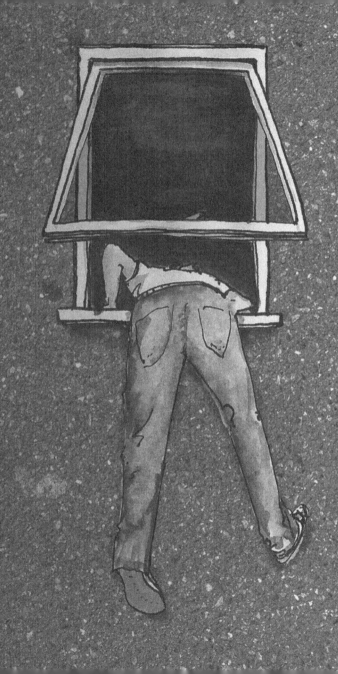

HOMERUN

I like running. I run to work. I run home from work. I don't
bother getting changed. It's not that sort of running. I just run
to get to where I'm going quicker. When I run home I run even
faster. I can't wait to get home. Home is where the kids are,
watching something on television. Home is where the wife is,
doing something in the kitchen. By the time I get to my street,
I've built up quite a sweat. I sprint up the pavement. My wife is
there at the door. Take your shoes off, she says.

RAMUS
RAMUS

Ramus Ramus is an old devil. His hair is grey, his back is bent, his knees are large, and he walks with the aid of two sticks. Ramus Ramus is getting old - except, of course, for his face. For it is plain to see that Ramus Ramus has the face of a young man. His nose is small and his eyes are bright, and when he laughs his teeth shine like the sun. Whenever you see Ramus he is happy and he is surrounded by women half his age. Has nobody else noticed this? Ramus Ramus is an old devil.

EVERY TIME WE SAY GOODBYE

Every time we say goodbye, my friend and I do a special handshake. We do a high five, then a side five, a knuckle touch and a heel click. My friend and I have had our special handshake since school, and even though he works in a bank, and I've been in the army, and he's married, and I've lived in places like Naples and the Fiji Islands, we still do it. Only now my friend has added a bum stroke to the special handshake. It's a good move. We do it a lot, even when we're not saying goodbye.

FAIR TRADE

My friend Makali Kerwanty lives on the side of a mountain in Ethiopia. He grows coffee. Once the site of continuous conflict, the introduction of controlled plantations has brought peace to the region. What's more, the coffee is licensed as fair trade, meaning Makali's business benefits from ethical market forces. Last week, I saw Makali's coffee for sale in the supermarket. There is a picture of him smiling on the packet. I was just about to buy some when I noticed that the fair trade coffee from Guatemala was almost a pound cheaper. So I bought that instead. Sorry Makali.

THE END

Marcus F Shepherd, otherwise known as The End, such is his capacity for bringing what was once a lively and interesting conversation to an abrupt close, is coming to my house this afternoon, at one o'clock, in two minutes, which is why, as you can see, I am trying to say as much as humanly possible, because, when he arrives, wearing, as per usual, and whatever the weather, an overcoat, a bandana and sunglasses, I will be rendered completely and utterly incapable of speaking another word. He will say: Stop all that talking - now. And I will. I promise.

ONE HUNDRED WORDS OF THANKS

Thanks and much love to our families, to Tash and Otto (Waddell), to Vicki, Bobbie and Milly (Felstead). Thank you for the music Barry 'the Bazooka' Foster. Thanks Tara Gould for the Short Fuse stage. Thanks for *Snapshot* Louise Hume, Lee Thacker and Dave Gedge. Thanks to Damian Barr for all the Charleston glory. Thanks to Colin Grant and Jo Alderson for Speaky Spokey. Thanks for the design Charlie De Grussa. Thanks for publishing us Robbie McCallum. Thank you friends and family for beefing up the Felstead and Waddell support. You have let us behave very badly. We are grateful.

Felstead and Waddell live in Brighton, UK. They write stories. Each story is 100 words long. They perform their 100 word stories. They wear wigs and suits and things.
→ felsteadandwaddell.co.uk

Lightning Source UK Ltd.
Milton Keynes UK
UKOW07f1927221114

242025UK00009B/84/P